OLIVIA™
Trains Her Cat

adapted by Sarah Albee, based on the screenplay
"Olivia and Her Trained Cat" written by Joe Purdy
illustrated by Shane L. Johnson

Ready-to-Read

Simon Spotlight
New York   London   Toronto   Sydney

Based on the TV series *OLIVIA*™ as seen on Nickelodeon™

SIMON SPOTLIGHT
An imprint of Simon & Schuster Children's Publishing Division
1230 Avenue of the Americas, New York, New York 10020
For information about special discounts for bulk purchases, please contact Simon & Schuster Special Sales
at 1-866-506-1949 or business@simonandschuster.com.
Manufactured in the United States of America 0710 LAK
First Simon Spotlight hardcover edition August 2010
2 4 6 8 10 9 7 5 3 1
The Library of Congress has cataloged the paperback edition as follows:
Albee, Sarah.
Olivia trains her cat / adapted by Sarah Albee ; illustrated by Shane L. Johnson. — 1st ed.
p. cm. — (Ready-to-read)
"Based on the TV series, Olivia as seen on Nickelodeon"—Copyright page.
ISBN 978-1-4169-8296-8 (pbk) (alk. paper)
I. Johnson, Shane L, ill. II. Olivia (Television program) III. Title.
PZ7.A3174Ol 2009
[E]—dc22
2009011862
ISBN 978-1-4424-1383-2 (hc)

My cat,  , can jump,"

says  .

GWENDOLYN

FRANCINE

"Wow!" all of the kids say.

"And  can also

GWENDOLYN

walk on her back legs,"

says  .

FRANCINE

"My cat, , can dance

EDWIN

ballet!" says  .

OLIVIA

"Wow!" all of the kids say.

can cook," says .

GWENDOLYN

FRANCINE

"So can !" says .

EDWIN

OLIVIA

"Your  sound special," says .

MRS. HOGGENMULLER

"Can you bring your

CATS

for show-and-tell?"

"We can have a
pet talent contest!" says  .
OLIVIA
"Great idea!" says .
MRS. HOGGENMULLER
"Everyone can bring a pet!"

" just likes to sleep,"
EDWIN

says .
JULIAN

"Will do tricks?"
EDWIN

 is sure that will.
OLIVIA   EDWIN

"Okay,  EDWIN , jump!" commands OLIVIA .

EDWIN keeps sleeping.

"If you jump through this ○ HOOP , you can have a FISH !"

EDWIN just snores.

"Is something wrong,  OLIVIA ?"

asks  MOTHER.

" EDWIN will not do tricks!"

says  OLIVIA sadly.

"He just sleeps!"

"It is hard to get an old CAT
to do tricks," says  MOTHER.

"But FRANCINE has a CAT that
will do tricks!" groans OLIVIA.

The next day at school,
the talent show begins.
"My  can eat
HAMSTER

a 🥕," says 🐷 .
CARROT   DAISY
Everyone claps.

"My 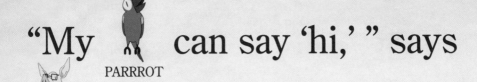 can say 'hi,' " says

PARRROT

.

HAROLD

"Hi, there!" says the 🦜 .

PARROT

Everyone claps.

"This is my 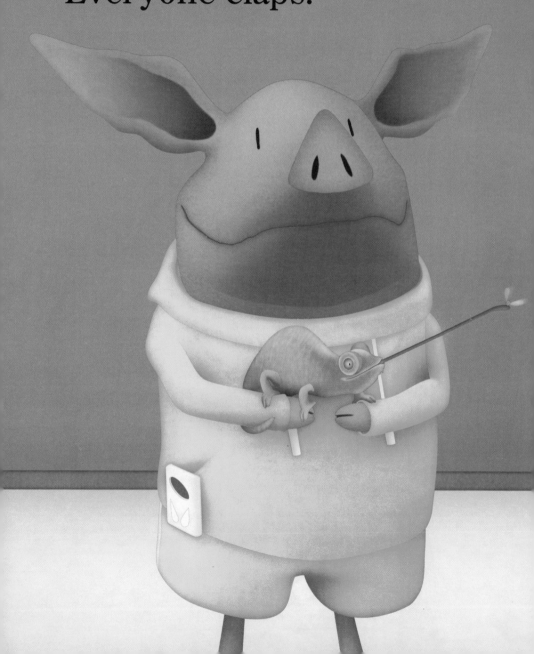," says   .
LIZARD   JULIAN

"He can catch a   ."
                     FLY

Everyone claps.

"This is my cat, ,"
EDWIN

says  .
OLIVIA

" can do many tricks."
EDWIN

"Jump,  !" says Olivia.

EDWIN

 sleeps.

EDWIN

Oh, no! Olivia worries.

"Okay, then, sleep, 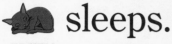!"

EDWIN

 sleeps.

EDWIN

"Now, snore, !"

EDWIN

 snores.

EDWIN

Everyone claps.

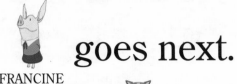 goes next.

FRANCINE

"Meet ."

GWENDOLYN

She can walk on her back  .

LEGS

She can flip backward.

She can jump

through a  .

HOOP

"I think we have a winner!

The winner is  !"

GWENDOLYN

says .

MRS. HOGGENMULLER

After school  OLIVIA
and JULIAN go to her HOUSE.
" EDWIN should have won,"
says JULIAN.

She looks around.

"Where is ?"

OLIVIA and JULIAN

search and search.

 and  go
OLIVIA   JULIAN

to 's  .
FRANCINE   HOUSE

They find  .
GWENDOLYN

They also find  doing tricks!
EDWIN